the dog, the voice & the side road

ALEX MASCARENHAS

the dog, the voice & the side road

Copyright © 2012 by Alex Mascarenhas

Cover Design: Jaia Papitz & Alex Mascarenhas

Cover Photo: Jaia Papitz

ISBN: 978-0-9858881-2-1

I dedicate this book – my first – to the ones who have always supported me, and whose infinite love and patience have nurtured me even from afar, no matter what the circumstances:

my mother, D. Waldith, and my father, S. Luiz.

(and I do mean infinite patience)

Dedico este livro – meu primeiro – àqueles que sempre me apoiaram, e cujo amor e paciência infinitos têm me estimulado mesmo de longe, quaisquer que sejam as circunstâncias:

minha mãe, D. Waldith, e meu pai, S. Luiz.

(e haja infinita paciência)

Acknowledgements

This book had at its inception a dare — albeit a most friendly one. As I was leaving on a long journey, my brother in arms J.P. put forth the challenge (invitation?) that I should "return with a novel" — and thus that was the catalyst for this... novel.

Contents

"Made up my mind to make a new start
Going to California with an aching in my heart
Someone told me there's a girl out there
With love in her eyes and flowers in her hair"

Led Zeppelin's "Going to California"

PROLOGUE

It's hard to say — or even realize — what the bottom of the well looks like.

Most people, I assume, haven't seen the bottom of the well. I haven't — at least not the degradation variety of bottom of the well. What I had a glimpse into was the vertigo of emotional bottom, and moments when you watch yourself in disbelief and think: "What is my fucking problem?"

I think I have problems. Yes, problemS — plural. Oh, I think I have so many problems.

I have no physical or mental handicaps — although some of my friends have at times questioned the veracity of the latter. I have a loving and absolutely supportive family. I have friends that don't bullshit me. I have a job that I bitch about. I have a certain amount of talent for one or two things of the artistic persuasion that have not brought me any recognition or fortune, but have at times entertained others. I had the unconditional love of a woman which became conditional due to my own human condition and my utter inability to foresee contingencies until they reached a continental scope.

You see, I think I have problems. Lots of problems.

I do have one problem – it seems I broke something. Or, perhaps, I am that something... Yesterday I thought it was time to finally tend to the problem.

I watched the sky as yesterday became today. Now is today.

Today I must go try and fix a thing or two.

I have had the privilege to meet a few wise souls – some of them residing in aged oak barrels; some in ageless architectonic edifices. To be the loving target of their mind dazzles one's own. They speak so plainly that you think: "How didn't I see that?" And they speak in winding descents, bending the language, and you think: "How did he see that?" In both cases, the arrow is delivered with lively precision to its target – bulls-eye, no two ways about it. In both cases, they speak so brilliantly that they force-feed you the light. If your eyes had been closed as you enjoyed the barrage of discernment coming your way, you'd better have them opened when the flickering torch at the end of the tunnel shows itself. To you. Make no mistake about it – it is showing itself to *you.*

I have done wrongs. Some, I can fix. Is it possible to make all wrongs right? Do the wronged wish to be righted?

Many years ago, as I sat on a bus going home from school, these two guys I knew sat in the seat right in front of mine. We all spoke the same language natively, but they came from another country to attend college in my motherland and, as it happens, also spoke a dialect which was intertwined with the idiom we shared. As they talked to each other, I could get the gist of what they were saying, but certain things uttered seemed completely foreign to me (I wasn't aware of those guys' idiomatic mixing powers, you see – those two bastards).

I've had these instances when, for a brief moment, I think I'm losing my shit and my mind has fully abandoned me – how can I hear something, understand it, and not know all that's really being said? Or is it hearing a few known words and presuming to understand what's being meant? Am I a great understander, or does the meaning of things elude me? Is it brief insanity? Or is it brief lucidity?

Yesterday I arrived at the site where I'm supposed to

[3]

be – my first station, anyway. A full month has already gone by. The first leg of the trip being over, now the journey begins. I have a mission: I have been commissioned to write a novel in the next eighty days or so. It'll be my first novel. Even if it's not a novel novel, I will call it so. It will be written.

I. Will. Right. It.

CHAPTER I

A man is born. Not yet a man, obviously, but a fragile, one-hundred-per-cent-full-of-hope-and-bright-future unit similar to many others arriving that same minute, like trillions of units already brought into obsolescence and made out-of-stock over the eons. His time is already running out, one grain of sand after the other; his clock has already started ticking — tic, tic, tic. Run, little man, run.

There was once a boy who lived in a barn. His companions were a huge dapple gray horse and a white yet black-masked mongrel dog; he sported a low-hanging holster cradling a six-shooter, toted a Winchester rifle, and... what else... Oh, and he donned a black hat and worn-out boots. This is the life he had chosen. This was the choice for his first incarnation.

Life was simple then. He had all he needed in his barn. And when he was hungry, he would hunt in the wild grounds, he would fish from the ocean just four hundred miles away. He never needed help in any way, as some four guys had said a bit earlier.

The Boy wasn't afraid of monsters – in fact, he was keen on seeking the sight of them. And monsters then were everywhere. He would look outside his window on the upper deck of his barn, and there they were; he saw them on micro billboards spottable through the telescope device of his trusty hunting rifle (the Winchester was a hybrid); they spoke in roaring, deafening growls, but he knew their language well and knew to enjoy their company or blast them to hell – whichever was suitable. And he had an ally – he didn't wear a hat himself, but then again, he had egg eyes and a square metal chin, and he was a silver rubber-clad giant.

Keep in mind that you cannot rhyme eight-year-old and fear-of-something – it's a mystical impossibility.

Some beasts met him with an open heart – and he walked right in there, where crimson knowledge washed away doubts, and winding channels led to yet more searching – the kind that sometimes remains without reasoning.

Unanswered questions had begun to stack up just beneath the hay.

The Boy's barn was adorned with all kinds of graphic motifs on the unsuspecting, yet grateful, canvasses. And colors abounded, although he was mostly partial to shades of onyx. And he lived on his barn for quite some time, until one day he awoke and he wasn't in his barn anymore. Better yet, his barn was no longer there. Although the real truth might be that he killed all the monsters he had set out to battle against and, thus, his life ended. That life ended.

CHAPTER 2

There would be a job search in New York City, and The Boy, now reincarnated, must be well to befit the challenges which lie ahead. He must train. Heroes have missions; the super ones have likewise super ones.

A two-year lifetime of seemingly relentless preparation for the daunting task ahead, a less-than-severe regimen for all-but-average physical performance, autodidact homeschooling on both ancient and contemporary martial practice. Becoming a hero isn't easy; make it a super one, and it becomes super uneasy for one's expectations. Expectations. Expectations. Expectations. Such a lovely word.

And the Small Dragon wasn't born — not in China, anyway, where the little one wished at some point that his parents would've wedded and conceived him. A fire-breather he was, albeit one with a youthful whim left unfulfilled.

He walks across the kitchen; his pace is swift. Out the door, over the railing; the horizon meets verticality as he descends through the air; touchdown – smoothly, firmly. He looks around. He is a spider.

The spider's grown fast; wants to expand the boundaries of his web-making. Now, if one can make a big apple, one can make anything. Fruit for thought.

Meanwhile, The Boy is also adept at putting pencil to paper. He enjoys fancy cars, fast horses, sexy six-shooters, un-urban spurs, unadorned Jeeps, stylish motorcycles, uncouth hats, dirty boots, ancient Eastern fighting, agile flying fighters. And he's good at making them appear from the tip of a graphite stick. Well, New York is where the heroes live; it's also lair for the ones who give them life. A couple of far away options; so many alternatives, so little time lived. The Big Apple will have to wait.

How many lives does one live? Well, this particular one has come to a screeching halt.

He was the walrus.

One could learn an entire language swiftly in the (much earlier) afore-mentioned fashion. Right? I think I think so. Bullshit! A language is more than a handful of memorized words; a life is more than a handful of memorized memories. Much, much more. Or is it? How many memories does one have? How many memories would one take to a deserted island? Which ones? Is a sweet memory that makes you cry worth taking to a sea of sand? To a sea of water? Would you leave all your bitter memories behind? Or do you crave them more than you do bliss?

The answers you have – or lack – for questions everyone asks tell people who you are. But do the answers you have or lack tell *you* who you are?

⁓◦⊱✦⊰◦⁓

At the onset of today's shining star I awake to the realization of my soulless existence. This has become a daily occurrence. It's easier to live without it when you're unaware of its absence. You don't miss what you never really had before (or didn't know you had acquired), the same way you don't miss a second nose on your face. What's the point of a flower growing out of your chest? Well, make damn sure you have had (or haven't had) one – and be reeeally sure – before rushing to hasty conclusions.

The Whole

I went to bed one night, the same way I went to bed all nights before that one. The next day, I started walking around with a pearl floating on my chest – just like that. I found it pretty, very, very pretty, and left it there, and peaked at it every now and then. Soon, I noticed that it was beginning to become larger. I was becoming richer. However, I had never been rich before, and that oversized former little pearl was now halfway lodged *in* my chest; it should hurt, but, instead, it felt good. So good, in fact, that it challenged my senses, my logic.

Well, I hadn't been rich before, and could not deal with my now expanding riches – even worse, that single pearl was spawning smaller ones all over my chest. I was a shell choking on the expansion of beauty. I started to spit out whatever I could – *I gotta breathe!* Others around me started to collect what I dismissed, what I rejected. That which I expelled out of my chest. That round, perfect life form I wouldn't allow to cover me, and to take over. "All the same to me", I reasoned. "Those tiny pearls were pretty, but I feel more comfortable now."

And the pearls used to roll on my chest and

neighboring adjacencies – all over, really – and that tickled me. It became a habit – picking them up and tossing them with the flick of a finger, the way you do a marble. Mindlessly, I started to pick at the mother pearl. She had long become embedded in me, and I began to sort of dig around it, eventually working my digging under that huge, marvelous pearl.

One day – and I'm not certain how it happened – I woke up, and I was in excruciating pain. I ripped my shirt open, and there it wasn't... I see no blood, but I feel it dripping from me. There's a gaping hole where my pearl used to be. The pain becomes acute as I search for my pearl, first feigning calm – feigning both to myself, and for the benefit of flies on the wall –, trying to keep my bearings; progressively, the area around the aching hole feels numb, deadened – but not the hole. The hole is well alive. Life in death isn't incongruous – it's but an afterthought. The hole had become me, as I became the hole.

I put on a shirt to cover it but, implausibly, the crater sticks out, protruding, and others notice the bulge on my chest where it's enormously concave. I put on an overcoat for protection against inquisition; then an armor. But then again, people tend to notice armors. Anyway, the armor is made of glass, gray and semi-opaque glass; and whatever light comes in from the outside... it gets inside, well, grayish and pale. And, as the light is reflected back outside, it now shines back black.

That was yesterday.

This is today. This is at 3:02 pm.

⁓꙳⁓

⁓꙳⁓

Friday. I'm at a new location, but it's very familiar surroundings. However, I feel encased — just as much as I felt elated exact four hundred and fifty days prior. The moon then shone in here as bright as sunshine.

⁓꙳⁓

I've been reading a book. This book speaks of connecting dots. I'm enjoying this non-fiction (although sometimes its nature seems otherwise) piece of literature, yet I've been ADD-ing, trying to connect dots as I read and constantly losing focus. No, wait. No, that's not accurate. I have been trying *not* to connect dots as I read. And I also have been trying *not* to connect dots as I walk. I have been trying *not* to connect dots as I eat. I have been trying *not* to connect dots as I speak to people or even sleep.

[13]

I had a fall some time ago. Months. A year. Could it be longer? A few minutes ago, even. I fell on my face. Have you ever fallen on your face? At first, you're not sure what just happened — it occurred too quickly, and you usually don't see it coming. "What is happe...?" Bam — ground. And you hear a horrible noise inside of your head as your face makes contact with the Earth, and for the briefest of seconds you realize: "I just smashed my one face on something very real and very hard, and it's breaking completely as I think this thought." You get up, somewhat dazed, confused. A painful awareness washes over you, and you don't really want to touch your face — you could make it worse; you don't want to come in touch with the reality of your circumstance. Zero acknowledgment equals zero actuality — the unerring math of denial. But then you want to see the damage, inspect how bad your predicament really is; and you go after a mirror. Now, you don't want to look in the mirror, not really — let's face it (yeah, pun), it's scary; you're not quite sure what you'll see, but you're pretty certain it won't be good. You stand there and make an attempt at appeasing your racing mind as it barrels down Desperation Road. "Look on the count of three: One... You're breathing too heavily — calm down, man. Easy. Yeah, like that... good. Now, take a deep breath. Two... and... three — open your eyes!" Surprisingly, it doesn't seem that bad. "You lucky bastard!" Of course, had your face had vital organs, this would've been one of those internal injuries kind of accidents – not that much damage on the outside, but a world of destruction where you can't really see it. And you don't – not for a while; and maybe you never see it at all. Maybe you never *see* it at all. What is it that they say? "Out of sight, out of mind." In the mind. Out of sight.

But I digress – as I often do.

The book I'm reading speaks of connecting dots to understand your circumstances, but you only see where they actually led – or, rather, you only see how you got where you now are – if you look back. In hindsight you perceive the dots as they interface with one another as in a reverse countdown: blastoff... 1... 2... 3... That first event – unseen/unnoticed/unremembered, as it may happen – ignited a chain reaction that crossed time and space, shaped events, moved moments and characters here and yonder – each a dot in its own right – as the plot wrote itself. And I can't deny it. It makes absolute sense.   And I can't deny it because I have been connecting fucking dots for six thousand hours, back and forth, and I seem to be always finding an overlooked dot – usually hidden in plain sight – that had eluded me, my grasp of how I chronicled – sometimes unfavorably – my own narrative, or let others shape it whenever I failed to look inwardly when searching for truth. Make no mistake: you have been building your own outcome from day one. And it's not a straight line – your trajectory, how you get there (wouldn't that be easy, fellas? Ladies?); and sometimes you trip, and sometimes you pretend to trip, and sometimes you even pretend you want to get up. Right now, this very moment, I'm on my knees; I'm on my hands and knees, crawling on the bottom of my own walls. I hope I get to be on my feet again.

I like what I just put to paper – "You have been building your own outcome from day one." How modest and honest of me, to not be covertly fond of my own words. Words to live by, nonetheless. Hmm... I wish I had nonethelessed this truism the day I was born.

I'm gonna stir things up somewhat before I hit the proverbial hay: what if... *what if* I meant "trip" in another sense?

What does this all have to do with writing a novel? Is this even a novel?

Hmm... I'll allow it seems iffy at times. Damn it! Well, I'm still calling it so. Just bear with me and have a little faith — not a whole lot to ask.

About that "trip" thing... I was just fooling around. This is a serious book.

CHAPTER 3

Once upon a time there was a boy who wanted to be a ballplayer. He already was a mythical entity revered in the East; eleven were his peers, but of a more-grounded-in-reality quality — that, however, has little to do with this tale, although this attribute makes for very popular tattoo motifs.

Let's just say that all boys wish to be ballplayers. You get the laurels, you get the riches, you get the girl. And, of course, you get to play ball. Likely, it's his very first calling. Likelier, it won't be the last. Likelier still, alas, it will be the last one he hears. Our ears pick up what we allow our eyes to catch a glimpse of — which is to say: a calling, to be heard, must first be perceived.

> Sometimes I wonder if, years from now (or days, even), I'll be capable of comprehending what now seems so evident — even if not blatantly overt. And I almost wish that I'm not.

But the life of a ballplayer is rather short, and most

are in fact so short that they never get to even bow out from the theatre of the mind.

Hmm...

The Theatre of the Mind — where most plots get written; where all actors are beautiful (except maybe for the one playing the iniquitous villain or the treacherous former lover — the latter having, no doubt, had a plastic falling from grace where looks are concerned); where our feats are romantic and absolutely daring; and where every single ending greatly favors the hero — ourselves — and is utterly Hollywoodian in the scope of its happiness-meter.

❧

Have you ever done something that, due to its lasting outcome and/or consequences, you wish you had never, ever done? Conversely, have you ever taken an action that absolutely gave your life the most positive of spins, and you've been since living the life you have always wanted? If not, try and think of something in a smaller scale, maybe. And if you can't come up with anything at all, well, then sit this one out. Anyhow, what I'm getting at is this: the two instances are one and the same.

Breaking it down to make my point:

In the first scenario, if you had *not* done what you did do, you wouldn't have to regret it – and you wouldn't, obviously, be privy to the particular outcome (and/or consequences) you now must endure. Who is to say, however, that something even more dire couldn't have been your end result from not having done that one (seemingly) "dreadful" thing? Clarifying: it's very possible that not having done what you did do could have put you in an even worse predicament than the one you came to find yourself in. What does that mean? It can only mean one thing: you probably did the best thing, the right thing back then – you indeed did what you needed to do in order to not really fuck your shit up. Does it make you feel any good to know this? Maybe not. Maybe not now – but wait until you wake up in the middle of the night with the realization that having smashed your TV screen with a kitchen hammer was stupid, yes, and now you can't watch TV anymore, but... On CNN (which you can't watch): *"Scientists have just discovered that those gamma rays from TV screens eventually lead to the melting of the left testicle in males and the greening of the labia majora in females."* Put that in perspective and you'll have a whole new appreciation for whatever perceived pickle life has served you as a result of your pointless gesture of obliteration.

Why dedicate a whole page to seeming nonsense?

Well, this is my feel-good-about-some-stupid-shit-that-you-did moment (or, alternatively, some bad shit that someone did to you and you felt wronged by the rotten individual – it is possible the jerk did you a favor). It could've turned out worse. Much worse. Cheers, then.

However...

The second scenario: you're living the life of your dreams because that one time you played your cards really well. Good for you. But did you really play it right? Maybe – just *maybe* – if you had folded your metaphorical cards, you'd be living the life you *never* dreamed of. Who knows what that could be – a life of even more abundant abundance; a life of unimaginable adventure and perils; a life of selfishlessness and complete unmaterialistic servitude to your fellow man; a life devoted to the subjugation of deadly diseases; even a life of absolutely unrestrained debauchery, indulgence and excess, so as to give the lives of the self-righteous some meaning.

Not so exultant about your dream life anymore? Didn't mean to rain on your parade, baby.

The two instances – one and the same. The randomness of living – when doing what's apparently wrong [maybe] works for the best, and doing what seems right [conceivably] fucks an endless well of possibilities.

Sweet stitch-snipper, bitter heart-snatcher. She's had my blood all over her hands, yet my skin sheathing her every inch.

CHAPTER 4

Street soccer. Growing up, that was a way of life (albeit a short-lived one – once you are finished growing up, so is the lifestyle). Well, you go to school – that's as far as your set formal schedule goes, along with whatever school stuff you must set time aside to work on – and the rest of the time was your time, and that usually meant getting with the boys and making art with a ball (yes, art sometimes happened – although you must know soccer to comprehend what I mean). Those were the times when girls didn't matter – and as passage of time and rites of passage would have it, right after that they would become everything that mattered.

You do anything for girls. You comb your hair for them. You spray on some deodorant before you leave for school, and you do it for them. You and your friend each steal a book from the school library to give to the same girl, even though she already has a fella – and you do that for them. You get into a skirmish and get the living shit kicked out of you – or you do the shit-kicking, maybe – and you do it for them. You don't have much gold to call your own, but nonetheless you buy a drink to that girl at the bar who you think looked at you with lust in her eyes – and you obviously and expectantly do it for them. Your penis has never made the acquaintance of a vagina before, but you play it cool when you finally convince a lady into spending some kama-sutra time with you, and you think you're doing it because of yourself – but you do it for them. And then, after you make your entrance, then, well... then you will do *anything* for them.

Yes, the greatest force in the universe: the Pussy Power. The everlasting, omniscient, ubiquitous power of the pussy. Make no mistake about it – it's a power so great that even a distinguished line of warrior women pursue the comforting harbor and peace of its source in others like themselves in rather anthropophagous fashion, as surely do all men – most to face off and reckon with it, some to emulate the swing and attraction of its iconic nature, a few simply vying to sport one of their own. The phallus is fine – feels good to be a proprietor and all – but as a symbol, I don't know... so you have some monument sticking up in the air (an obelisk or what have you), and then you have *all* that surrounds that stick – *that* is the omnipresence itself. That's the pussy. The Ultimate Surrounder. That, my friends... *that* is the power.

Anyway.

And so The Boy leaves behind the playground. He is now after bigger toys, interactive ones, breathing ones that will toy with him as well. Like all of his other incarnations before him, he dies — yes, I admit, this was a hasty event-succession timeline. The boy in the barn is defunct. The boy who would be headed for New York City is comatose. The boy who wanted to be a professional ball kicker has kicked the bucket.

So again he died and reincarnated. He grew quickly this time. His voice changed, and so did his interests. His aspirations mutated somehow. But his aspirations will never mutate as much as they will when he meets The Girl. But that hasn't happened. Yet. Prelude for thought.

❧

New York City is a fascinating town. You walk twenty blocks in Manhattan and everything around you changes — the architecture, the way people dress and conduct themselves, even the rats on the subway tracks seem to behave differently (the ones on the Upper East Side platforms are a bit uptight, whereas the ones in SoHo have a certain flair, and if you leave the island you'd better not fuck with the ones on certain Brooklyn stations). And by the way, if you go to New York, don't be foolish and think that the city is only Manhattan —

you'd be missing out on a whole lotta love by dismissing the other boroughs.

The city is quite simply as alluring as a place can be. If you go as a tourist, it can be breathtaking in what wonders it offers you to experiment. If you live there for a little while, it can be a fun mistress in what fun games it offers you to experience. If you live there long enough, it morphs into a loyal, kind and tough lover that can be very accepting in what it lets you offer her. If you make it there, you can make it anywhere – probably a very true postulation. Most, however, will not make it there – not as far as monumental ambitions are concerned. Even as far as some more humble and mundane ambitions are concerned, in fact. This city is like a Lamborghini – beautiful, fast, and yeah, it could kill you. Most people do not make it there; most people simply get by there – as most people do anywhere, simply.

Ahh, but the possibilities, the prospects, the latent opportunities, the potential... Fuck the odds, and fuck the probabilities! Vegas, baby! Vegas? Fuck Vegas – New York, baby!

Risk and reward. The higher the former, the bigger the latter. Right? Right, wrong, who cares? Generally speaking, if you must give something a try, you've got to do it, because you owe it to yourself to do it, and that's all there is to it. No "if-I-hads" should be your epitaph. "I-trieds" are much more suitable wordings for a tombstone, be it made of heavy and polished marble, or — especially — for one that's a makeshift piece of wood plank. And who the fuck said that the bigger reward has to do with riches, anyway, when your smiling soul claims otherwise as it clicks its otherworldly heels in the green meadows of the beyond? Well, loot for thought.

CHAPTER 5

Screenplay
by

John Doe Smithson IV

Based on the novel
(yes, novel, that's right)

The Dog, the Voice & the Side Road

First draft: 10/21/11
Current draft: 08/04/12

Dog, Voice & Side Road Productions
1 Love Street
(555)555-5555

INT. WRITING ROOM - AFTERNOON

A room. As WE PAN AROUND, we notice some
art on the walls -- pencil drawings
depicting avant-garde cars, Old West-era
revolvers, fighting super-heroes
drenched in bright colors -- things a
boy once conceived.

In the back of the room, a confessional --
with prison bars separating the two-sided
contraption -- looks out a large back
window overlooking a beautiful landscape.
A velvet-covered ottoman in the center has
a comfy leather armchair facing it.
Nearby, spiraling steps leading upstairs,
and a round wooden table with two decks of
cards sitting on its top, sided by two
chairs across from each other.

There are TWO MEN in the room, but we do
not see them.

                    ANALYST
          So you're a screenwriter?

                    THE MAN
          A lil' bit.

                    ANALYST
          Are you also an actor?

THE MAN
I thought I was.

ANALYST
Well, are you?

THE MAN
Yes.

ANALYST
Can you do any real writing as
well?

THE MAN
Can I do any reel writing?

ANALYST
This kind of wordplay only
works on paper.

THE MAN
I have been commissioned to
write a novel.

ANALYST
Are you writing it?

THE MAN
I don't know. I'm writing
something, but don't know
exactly what it is.

                    ANALYST
Not a novel?

                    THE MAN
I thought it was, in the
beginning.

                    ANALYST
And now?

                    THE MAN
It morphed.

                    ANALYST
Yes?

                    THE MAN
I gave the first few pages for
my father to read.

                    ANALYST
Do you usually do that?

                    THE MAN
I had never done that, as a
matter of fact.

                    ANALYST
Why now, then?

                    THE MAN
I told him I was writing, and
he wanted to know what it was.

I didn't want to paraphrase my
own writing...

                ANALYST
Why not? Isn't the source the
same -- meaning yourself?

                THE MAN
Yes, but the thing about writing
-- good writing, anyway, as far
as I'm concerned -- is also the
form, the choices you make
regarding the words you use, the
style -- or lack thereof --

                ANALYST
Do you see yourself as a good
writer?

                THE MAN
I get by.

                ANALYST
Give me the truth.

                THE MAN
Yes, I am good.

                ANALYST
Anybody else told you that?

                THE MAN
You sound like my father.

                    ANALYST
        Do I? Am I?

                    THE MAN
        You're confused.

                                INSERT:

The Man's hand, as he makes a notation
on his own notepad.

                                CUT TO:

The Analyst, looking somewhat puzzled
and intrigued, and most definitely
analytical.

                            CUT BACK TO:

The Man, as he looks up again, waiting
for his interlocutor to make his move.

                    ANALYST
        So, your novel.

                    THE MAN
        So I gave my father the first
        few pages I'd written. He
        called it a *mea culpa*.

                    ANALYST
        Did he?

                    THE MAN
          Yes.

                    ANALYST
          Do you?

                    THE MAN
          I can see his point.

A beat.

                    ANALYST
          So you say it's no longer a
          novel?

                    THE MAN
          I don't know. It changes all
          the time.

                    ANALYST
          That gives you more freedom,
          doesn't it? You don't need to
          tie yourself up to a single
          way of telling the story.

                    THE MAN
          You sound like me.

                    ANALYST
          Do I? Well, will you sell it?

                    THE MAN
          Will anyone buy it?

ANALYST
I would.

THE MAN
Thank you.

ANALYST
I'm curious.

THE MAN
I'm anxious.

ANALYST
That's why you're here.

THE MAN
What is here, anyway?

ANALYST
This is you writing room. Your
space. Are you happy here?

THE MAN
Yes. And miserable. And
hopeful. And broken --

ANALYST
Your scriptwriting is boring.
Talk, talk, talk. Nothing
happens except talk.

THE MAN
We're setting up the action.

ANALYST
Is this what they call
expository?

THE MAN
Hopefully not.

ANALYST
Wait. We? *We* are setting up
the action?

THE MAN
Yes.

ANALYST
Does this mean I'm also
boring?

THE MAN
Are you?

ANALYST
Are you?

THE MAN
At times. Are you afraid of
being boring?

ANALYST
Of course. Isn't everybody?

The Analyst analyses his last statement.
WE STAY on him for a bit.

                    ANALYST (CONT'D)
          I should be asking the
          questions.

                    THE MAN
          You need answers too.

                    ANALYST
          This is like a fucking Harold
          Pinter script.

                    THE MAN
          I love Pinter.

                    ANALYST
          So you do.

                    THE MAN
          So I do.

A beat.

                    ANALYST
          I wish you were writing an
          action movie.

                    THE MAN
          We.

                    ANALYST
          We.

                                        FADE OUT.

It's possible I have been lying. To the one person I can't lie to.

Lying. Pretty easy thing to do, if you think about it. Say whatever untruths you must (and sometimes you really must) with a bit of conviction, and move on with the conversation. Kind of say it in passing. Or make it a half-truth – it's not a lie if there's some truth in it. These are the best ones, because you feel good – rather, you don't feel bad – about yourself; you're not a [complete] impostor, you're not [really] dishonest, it wasn't [quite] cheating. Yes, it's not a lie if there's some truth in it. It just stands to reason. Someone is not dead if there's some life left in them. Right? Right. If there's some truth in it, it's not a lie. It just stands to reason. You can't argue with reason. And that's how you do it – you keep telling it to yourself. Obviously, if you can find some justification (for yourself, the liar, not for the liee – fuck the liee) so much the better. In fact, that helps a lot. I mean, who wants to carry the burden of acknowledging he's a liar, of perpetuating a lie which might need indefinite continuation? Too much to bear. And too much fucking work, come to think of it. Find yourself a good justification, or even a so-so reason for your tiny slip, and that goes a long way toward an excuse from a guilt trip. Half-truths, quarter-truths, one-percent-truths... Got a drop of truth in a couple of gallons of, uh... non-truth? Good enough. Lying to oneself could be a bitch, though — the old "you can lie to some people some of the time, and you can lie to a lot of people a lot of the time, but you cannot lie to all people all..." No, wait, this is another one... In any case, in lying to oneself, one, for good measure, should throw in a few more drops of truth. Yep, that should do. Dilute for thought.

Anyway, it has been a few days since I last put words to virtual paper — at least where it concerns this particular endeavor — and it's been two full months since I wrote the first paragraph. The pace and content — not to mention the plot (aaaha!) — of my stream-of-consciousness novel has at times (constantly, to be quite honest) eluded me. It has eluded me, in fact, to the point that I'll have to go back and see where I have left my one principal character — my protagonist, as it were...

Well, then...

When one finds The One, one's life changes somewhat. If one loses The One, one will change inexorably. Being the same simply isn't in the cards. Going back to being the same will not happen. One will lose oneself, possibly miss oneself, and be irrefutably certain that their paths – the current self's and the former self's – will never again cross.

You fucked up? She deceived you? She lied? You believed? You hurt her? She caused you pain? You were good? She was better? You told the truth? She heard what she wanted? You wounded her? She killed you? You let her go? She abandoned you? You were in denial? She moved on? All of the above? Well, well, well... One will change. Inexorably.

CHAPTER 6

The Boy. And he grew up tall, but did he grow up right?

And he used to walk by seashores where mermaids lured sailors, and wooded mountains where Artemis protected runaway minotaurs, and valleys where silicone princesses lost their virtue, and lakes where gigantic oaks sprouted from the bottom and bowed over swimming virgins to shield them from the moonlight above. And thus The Boy was swallowed by hungry mermaids, and befriended extraordinary minotaurs, and deflowered his share of princesses, and blocked cool silver beams of light.

And life was good. Better, in fact, than The Boy cared to realize, too busy that he was committing to life itself — and to little else besides. And not once did he ever wake up and ponder what a good day that might be to die. Life was rock 'n' roll. The blues was still nowhere in sight.

But then the mermaids could no longer satiate him; the minotaurs he now deemed unremarkable; the virgins stepped down to whoredom; and who needs shading from moonlight, anyway?

And so he left. And he did leave it all behind.

The Meaning. The Meaning. The Meaning.
The Meaning. The Meaning. The Meaning.
The Meaning. The Meaning. The Meaning.
The Meaning. The Meaning. The Meaning.
The Meaning. The Meaning. The Meaning.
The Meaning. The Meaning. The Meaning.
The Meaning. The Meaning. The Meaning.
The Meaning. The Meaning. The Meaning.
The Meaning. The Meaning. The Meaning.
The Meaning. The Meaning. The Meaning.
The Meaning. The Meaning. The Meaning.
The Meaning. The Meaning. The Meaning.
The Meaning. The Meaning. The Meaning.
The Meaning. The Meaning. The Meaning.
The Meaning. The Meaning. The Meaning.
The Meaning. The Meaning. The Meaning.
The Meaning. The Meaning. The Meaning.
The Meaning. The Meaning. The Meaning.
The Meaning. The Meaning. The Meaning.
The Meaning. The Meaning. The Meaning.

The Meaning. The Meaning. The Meaning. The Meaning. The Meaning. The Meaning. The Meaning. The Meaning. The Meaning. The Meaning. The Meaning. The Meaning. The Meaning.

I was watching a film with Philip Seymour Hoffman. "I'll remember this for the rest of my life. In twenty years..."

The Meaning. The Fucking Meaning.

CHAPTER WHAT ?

Screenplay
by

John D. Smithson

Based on the novel
(I sometimes have my doubts too...)

The Dog, the Voice & the Side Road

First draft: 11/10/11
Current draft: 11/10/11

Dog, Voice & Side Road Productions
1 Love Street
(555)555-5555

EXT. AN OPEN PATIO AT A BAR - NIGHT

A large patio near a fountain. People
are sitting in deuces and scattered
around in small groups, drinking,
smoking, talking, laughing, cavorting.
The indistinct sound of unknown voices
and blues music playing in the
background.

A bar to one side, and patrons yelling
their orders. On the other side, a big
oak tree, surrounded by a knee-high
bench-like brick fence.

Under the oak, THE MAN and THE WOMAN
have just met, but know each other since
before they were born.

                    THE WOMAN
          Do you come from a far away
          land?

                    THE MAN
          Can you tell?

                    THE WOMAN
          Yes. Well, do you?

                    THE MAN
          Yes.

THE WOMAN
I come from a far away galaxy.

THE MAN
I can tell you descended from
the sky.

THE WOMAN
Can you? What gave me away?

THE MAN
The tips of your wings are
showing.

Beat.

THE WOMAN
Clever. Albeit mundane.

THE MAN
Mundane you're not.

THE WOMAN
Touché!

THE MAN
Why are you here tonight,
under this oak tree?

THE WOMAN
I came to be in its shade.
Besides, I've flown enough,
and my wings need rest.

Beat.

                    THE WOMAN (CONT'D)
          What do you do?

                    THE MAN
          I chase pussy.

                    THE WOMAN
          Indeed?

                    THE MAN
          I'm a pretty proficient tree
          climber. I work for the City
          rescuing little kittens from
          big trees.

                    THE WOMAN
          A lot of work lately?

                    THE MAN
          Too many neighborhood dogs
          keeping the pussy element
          indoors, actually.

                    THE WOMAN
          I see. I have a little kitten
          of my own.

                    THE MAN
          Little, is she?

He moves closer to her.

                    [47]

                    THE MAN (CONT'D)
          Does she purr?

She moves her head purposefully, puts
her lips to his ear, and lets out a low,
lewd, lingering purr.

X.C.U. ON HIS EYES.

                    THE MAN (CONT'D)
          Oh, goodness...

X.C.U. ON HER LIPS.

                    THE WOMAN
          Goodness is right...

Their eyes are so near one another's
that the world has ceased to exist. He
can feel her warm and moist breath; she
senses his lips pulsating.

She speaks under her breath.

                    THE WOMAN (CONT'D)
          What brought you here tonight?

They both speak now in a very low tone.
And it just gets lower...

                    THE MAN
          It was imperative that I came
          here tonight. I have yearned
          to be here this moment.

Their tongues are mute. Their souls
whisper to one another...

                    THE WOMAN
          You just knew I had to be here
          tonight.

                    THE MAN
          You just knew.

Her breath meets his lips.

                              FADE OUT.

Nude for thought.

Hyding Jekyll. Gooding evil. Spent my unkind kind of days with a kind kind of unkind woman. Wickedness uprightness vice righteousness virtue right wrong meanness honesty integrity venomousness deceit spitefulness decency rectitude corruption perversion purity baseness vileness kindheartedness turpitude viciousness innocence depravity respect amorality ruthlessness sin chastity clarity

I was at a party, a huge party. A huge house, a gorgeous, dazzling swimming pool, breathtaking gardens. Dozens, hundreds of people – the intelligent, interesting type. And some pretty good-looking too. Talking, laughter; discussions on politics, love, war, Mother Earth. Loud music, dance. Everybody seemed to know my name and they all wanted to talk to me, to meet me. Every single last one of them. I don't even know why. I mean, who the fuck wants to meet, to be friends with *everyone?* Well, maybe someone on Facebook. I only wished to see one person. The rest of them I just wanted dead. Out of the way. Vanished. They were of no importance. I wanted to see The One who dwells Below.

So I ask the bartender.

"Excuse me. I want to see The One who dwells Below."

"You sure 'bout the address?", he replies.

"I think so, yeah", I say.

"Then I don't know. Hold on." He turns to the other bartender. "Hey, Jim, Our Guy here is lookin' fo' The One who dwells... what is it again?"

"Below", I maintain.

"Yeah, Jim, Below, man."

"I don't know about that, Jack", the Jim fellow answers. "But The One Who Rules Above was asking about Our Guy there."

It turns out I'm the dude they seem to call Our Guy. And I wanted to see the Ruler From Above fella, but an appointment was needed – and I actually had one (in fact everybody does, sooner or later), but I wasn't willing to wait. I was desperate for answers. I was desperate.

I showed up early for my scheduled appointment with The One Who Rules Above. Many years early.

It's not true what I said, however. I liked to be

among all those people. I loved to listen to them talk because when their words filled my ears and my head I couldn't hear the flooding of my own rushing words screaming silently. I needed them to tell me their dreams so as to shield me from the shards of mine own.

I try again. Someone different this time.

"Excuse me. I'm looking for The One, who dwells Below."

"Are you sure about the address?" Are you serious? The same question to my inquiry? Really?

"Well, you know..." I begin to say. "You know what, I... She used to live in Syde Uvmee. She moved."

"Are you sure? She might still be living in there." At last. She knows who I'm talking about.

"She didn't like it there", I say. "She decided she could no longer live in Syde Uvmee."

"So how may I be of assistance?", she offers.

"The One Who Rules Above?", I inquire.

"Downstairs at the back, hon."

"Downstairs?", I muse. "Now *that* is interesting."

Days shorten as they get snoozed. And so weeks get snoozed – whole years, if you're not mindful. I'm not. I have so much I want to do. Most of it never leaves the winding confines of my head.

CHAPTER ELEVEN

Screenplay
by

J. D. S.

Based on the novel
(Not a novel? So why the screenplay?)

The Dog, the Voice & the Side Road

First draft: 11/??/11
Current draft: 07/17/12

Dog, Voice & Side Road Productions
1 Love Street
(555)555-5555

INT. T.O.W.R.A.'S PARLOR - NIGHT NOR DAY

OUR GUY has descended the steps leading
down to where he should find the one
with the answers he has been seeking.

This place isn't at all what he had
expected. The One Who Rules Above's den
is nothing more than a poolroom -- a
sizeable one at that -- with a bar at
one side, three or four dart boards on
other walls, about a dozen pool tables
scattered -- not lined up in rows -- on
the parlor's floor.

But the one thing that sets this
particular poolroom apart from any other
poolrooms you'd have seen are the spiral
staircases descending to a level below
or going up to the floor above -- except
that Our Guy didn't notice any of them
popping out upstairs.

Our Guy is greeted with a grunt from the
ENFORCER. He is a mountain of a fellow
with a long dark mane covering half of
his head -- the other half is completely
shaved and covered with tattoos. He
wears black clothes and a white trench
coat.

                    OUR GUY
I'm here to see The One Who
Rules Above.

                    ENFORCER
And who the fuck are you?

                    OUR GUY
Our Guy, they seem to call me.

                    ENFORCER
Well, friend, The One Who
Rules Above didn't ask you
here.

                    OUR GUY
He asked about me.

                    ENFORCER
Two different things.

                    OUR GUY
I need to see him. He might
have answers I've been
seeking.

                    ENFORCER
Do you know what time it is?

                    OUR GUY
No.

                    ENFORCER
          It's too early for you to see
          him.

                    OUR GUY
          Bullshit.

                    ENFORCER
          He's the bullshitter. You
          don't bullshit the
          bullshitter, son.

                    OUR GUY
          What if I make my own time?

                    ENFORCER
          That's obviously your
          prerogative.

                    OUR GUY
          I just chose to exercise it.

          The Enforcer grabs Our Guy by his
          collar, pulls him over the bar.

                    ENFORCER
          No you didn't.

          A voice descends the stairs.

                    T.O.W.R.A.
                      (O.S.)
          Yes, he did.

The Enforcer hurls Our Guy across the room.

                    ENFORCER
          You stupid fuck!

THE ONE WHO RULES ABOVE is middle-aged, and there's something at the same time paternal and thuggish about him. His hat and his boots are gray. His gray hair is long, and his face hasn't seen a razor in a week. He smells of gin and life.

                    T.O.W.R.A.
          I'll take over from here.

                    ENFORCER
          Be your own guest, Rules.

                    T.O.W.R.A.
                         (to the Enforcer)
          Why, thank you.
                         (to Our Guy)
          You had no business coming
          here to see me at this hour.
          But once you're here, take a
          swing at me.

Our Guy does. It smashes The One Who Rules Above square in the face.

                    T.O.W.R.A. (CONT'D)
          Felt good? Gimme another one.

Our Guy does.

                    T.O.W.R.A. (CONT'D)
          Here's one for you.

The One Who Rules Above then swings his
arm -- at least this seems to be what he
just did, for to actually see it is
impossible -- you just know it happened.
That sends Our Guy flying across the
room again. The One Who Rules Above gets
near him, and is met with a kick to the
nether regions.

                    T.O.W.R.A. (CONT'D)
          What, do you think I don't
          have balls? Well, I don't care
          what you think. And I'm gonna
          teach you a lesson, late as it
          may be.

He grabs Our Guy by the neck, shoves him
into a chair.

A beat.

He grabs another chair, places it across
from Our Guy's. He fishes for something
in the side pocket of his leather blazer
jacket, and produces a pack of smokes.
He very deliberately takes one to his
lips.

INSERT:

The Enforcer's hand enters the shot to light the boss' cigarette.

The One Who Rules Above takes a long drag off his cigarette, looks deeply into Our Guy's eyes.

                    T.O.W.R.A. (CONT'D)
          The One Who Dwells Below...
          You're seeking the wrong
          person. You're looking for a
          dead person, son. The Girl Who
          Lives Inside is who you are
          seeking, and she's been dead a
          long time.

                              FADE OUT.

I'm going to start taking care of my affairs, putting all of them in order, sorting out my personal affects, cleaning up my act, trying to rid myself of non-essentials — maybe not down to bare minimums, but streamlining. Maybe try to live every day as if it's the last. Because one day — and it could be near — it will be.

CHAPTER ???

Somewhere in a place between Hell and Heaven ("Hellven"?). It's very beautiful – eerie, some may say (well, the nay-sayers). The seas are purple, and when waves swell, they freeze so as to be ridden for hours, and then they crash exactly at midnight (whose midnight?) and shatter into tiny crystals that ascend instantly to the burgundy night sky, staying there floating, shimmering.

People are everywhere – on the white furry-carpeted beaches, in the glass coffeehouses suspended from gelatin trees, on the satin-blanketed mountaintops – and an idyllic serenity shines from them and permeates the air.

A strident feedback screech from a microphone echoes around. Out of a P.A. system, someone is heard clearing his throat. A bored voice calls out: *"John Doe."*

Without losing track of whatever their attention is directed toward, gazillions of voice owners reply in unison: "Which one?"

"The one with the girl issue", the voice announces.

Some trillions in unison: "Which one?"

"The one who blew his head off with a shotgun", the bodiless sound clarifies.

A few millions look up. In unison: "Which one?"

"The one who blew off the back *of his head."* End of story.

All: "Hey, Johnny!"

Someone yells back from a beach bungalow: "Yo!"

The bored voice out of the P.A. system summons: *"There's a girl here on the Séance Channel to see you."*

The crowd: "Uh-oh!"

Far in the distance, green snow shoots out of smiling volcano craters, stationing in midair so as to be rescued by the silvery beaks of blue-scaled birds zooming by.

Johnny Doe makes his way across the ethereal multitude with ease. Ease is the word of order in these parts. Everything moves and happens as in a Mozart symphony – effortlessly, smoothly, sans haste.

But The Girl. As she is ushered through meandering glass tunnels and up impossibly high escalators crossing quasi-opaque ceilings and sky-revealing transparent walls to the place of her meeting, The Girl seems unmoved by all the beautiful and, well, eerie circumstances surrounding her. No. No, that's not the case, really. She doesn't notice them. Her eyes are filled with the purpose she came here for. Even as a semi-glowing child with semi-catlike eyes sits her in what seems like a waterfall sofa – across from Johnny, who sits in a similar couch, facing her – she is not fazed.

"What the hell is that, Johnny?", she asks.

She refers to a... to something laying beside him on the couch.

"The back of my head", he replies. "Long story."

⚜

The two perfect, seemingly seamless halves of an orange. Ying and yang. Oneness. I'm keenly unaware of what the price for completeness is – and all I know is that, in the end, I unfortunately couldn't afford it. And I kept completely nothing from either half of the orange. Sued for thought.

Is it indeed truly possible to become more interested in the mysteries of the beyond than the sureties of the now? Does that make sense to the essence of human nature – to forgo the urgency of the flesh over the continuum of the unknown? What does it mean to "come out of it alive"? Is it feasible to come out alive, yet not living? Is any life – any life at all – taken with you when the mirror's surface no longer denounces your breath?

"Open the window, son", my father just proposed. "Let the soul in." I didn't say anything to him about my growing craving for releasing it instead.

December 21, 2012 – a little ways in the future. What a lovely prospect. Doom for the doomed. God for the God-seekers. The Wave, for the ones who dare ride it. The end of fear for the cowards. The ultimate challenge for the ones who think themselves brave. The end of nothing for the cynics who don't believe in anything at all. The non-beginning for the unborn and the long overdue comeuppance for the wicked. The possibilities are absolutely not endless.

❧

Skin; feet; hair; crooked smile; armpits; beauty mark; belly; smell. How can so much belong to just one being?

❧

I have been told she is dead. Yet she killed me.

❧

❧

❧

Writer's fucking block. I haven't touched this work in weeks. An entire month, really. Not really — exactly. Not written a page. Not a single word. A few scribbles, yes, on a couple of pieces of paper — that's about it.

Tonight will be Christmas Eve. Which reminds me that I haven't had Happy Times in a while. The occasional fun time, okay, yes — and it usually involves a certain amount of alcohol. A fair amount of alcohol.

Fun versus happy. In my own view: feeling good from the outside in (the former), as oppose to feeling good from the inside out (the latter). It's all about the tingling sensation, but here the source is what matters – and, of course, there's a lot to be said about having some good old fun, but if you ever were... if you ever felt happy... especially if you could share that with someone you loved... Fuuuuck! Then you will know the difference. Hmm... I reminisce, I suppose... This is very confessionary.

A year ago tonight I had an evening which foretasted hard lunar changes that brutally conspired – in the next hundreds and thousands of hours – to send my ship into a seemingly everlasting downright downward spiral.

It seems I could have stopped the dizzying turn of events had I said the wright words. Was there time to fix what didn't seem broken?

Five hours to Christmas. All but a week to a new year... Are you fucking kidding me? Another year of this shit? This nightmare? Spare me the agony. No, I'm not fucking joking, I'm pretty tired of the ticking of this particular clock.. 'Kay... Hmm... Is it too early – seven in the damn pm – and am I too sober for this climactic non-interlude? I haven't drunk a drop in weeks – although I absolutely intend to rectify this tonight. But for now I'll keep dry and go over my little notes – so buckle up.

My days feel like a deafening head-on collision with

[67]

nothing. At the wreck scene, nothing left to tell the story – only bits and pieces of... what? Some sweet memories and some bitter ones, fragments of... dreams... ideas... feelings... And there's pain, and there's numbness – I don't know which there is more of, which supersedes the other, or whether they have a mind of their own and in fact jockey for pole position. Nothing left at the scene, yet I walked away from the wreckage seemingly unscathed – people would ponder, anyway. "You're looking good." "Why, thank you." But my thoughts, my brain, my mind... it all feels like eggs as they are being scrambled. It *was* a head-on collision, after all.

Is this a diary? Has it become one? Well, I haven't touched it in a month, so at best it's a "monthly". My father – was he right, the old geezer? A *mea culpa?*

No, this is my novel. The most un-novel novel ever written, possibly. Why am I even writing it? Am I waisting my already emaciated time? Will I be misusing an eventual reader's time? A book should have a purpose – I'll re-phrase: a book worth reading should have a purpose – even if it's simply to entertain. I don't suppose most books – or most works of art – have a meaningful message attached. I mean, if it's there, so much the better... but my point is: do I have a point?

Am I just jabbering on, or will I be able to connect with people through these words? And does it matter, or did it matter when I started? Will I make any sense to others, when sometimes I struggle to piece together my own specks of thinking? And, in making sense to others, will I be of assistance in any fashion — I mean, will my writings serve any purpose, or be of any use? And again, does it matter? Clearly I won't offer any answers, for I in fact put forth more questions — my own — than propose elucidation. Too many questions. Am I losing sight of the mainland? Have I seen a mirage in the ocean? However, I am actually very fond of certain passages here, some of which I find quite entertaining... Fuck me! I am now becoming the critic of my own work — and giving myself a fairly benevolent review at that! It is now nearing 11:00 pm and I am working pretty diligently at obliterating my sober status. I'm doing a good job. Merry Christmas! Ho, ho, ho! Blued for thought.

Wait... what did I write last night? "Would my words be of any assistance to others?" What am I now, the Messiah? And on Christmas Eve, no less? Jesus, great timing, man... [1]

---

[1] No, I was not talking to Jesus... I meant *my* timing. Oh, well...

"A tormented artist's soul's slow descent into madness..." It sounds like an enticing Hollywood movie's tagline. Has anyone ever said to you that they might be losing their mind, and meant it? Have *you* ever felt like that — at the brink of sanity? You're alone, your thoughts crowding your thinking, which gets in the way of your thoughts, and it's so loud in your head that you can't hear yourself think... and you ponder: Am I in control here? *Is there* any control here? "I think, therefore I am." "Crazy people don't realize they're crazy. So, if I think that I might be crazy, then I'm not." Logic. Crazies can't do logic. The ability to rationalize excuses one from madness. It's logic. Meanwhile, logic is a mental process, and the Hollywood movie tagline clearly stated *"soul's* slow descent into madness..."

My dad's a jokester, and he's always having his fun at my mom's expense:

"When I married your mother — he says this at the dinner table —, she didn't know how to do anything. I asked her to fry me an egg, and she replied: 'What side of the egg do I break?'" My mom, sitting across the table from my dad, and not to be fucked with, shot back: "Yeah, but I did know what side of your face to break — both." They kill me.

⬥

This just in (well, perhaps not really *just* in...):

"Sometimes I feel like I'm standing at the very edge of reality. Like if I slipped I'd be gone. My mind would be gone. Something funny goes on inside my mind, deep inside my mind sometimes. Feels like I'm losing grasp of reality. That's the edge of the cliff I'm standing on. Then again, I think that, if I had lost my mind, I wouldn't be able to realize that. Mad people don't think of themselves as mad, I guess. I think, therefore I'm not mad. Yet. Funny thoughts. That's what people do when they have nothing else to do. I'd better get busy."

...as well as this:

> "I guess people have to get older to be able to realize certain things. I remember things that my dad used to say when he drank. Things that really pissed me off. At those moments, I almost hated him. I guess I thought I knew what he was talking about. Well, maybe I did, indeed. But I couldn't understand it. I hadn't lived quite enough, or at least gone through things he had, perhaps bad experiences with people. Unfortunately, I think now I have. I'm a grown man now, with all the bad things that come with it, and just a few, maybe even none, of the good ones."

I mentioned before that I've been commissioned to write a novel (that *is* what this is) by a good friend whose couch I'll be crashing on in a few days — I've been spending time in a distant land close to my heart these last few months, as I formerly imparted. Or, maybe, on second thought, I only divulged part of my current circumstances... Oh, well. Thing is: going through some old writings I encountered here (here being my parents' home, where I am in a critical transitional juncture, thousands of miles away from the place I have called home for the past ten years), I came across a piece of paper with the above two paragraphs, written in longhand. Now, had this been a computer file, I would probably know exactly when I wrote the stuff. That not being the case, I could only try and infer — based on whatever evidence I could gather from the writings themselves and some scribbling on the back of that page — when it was that I actually put ink to paper. It was some fifteen years ago. I found that sheet of paper in a box, quite simply. Now, the resemblance between this first paragraph quoted above and the one I wrote only two days ago on the page preceding that is astonishing. But said resemblance, coupled with the coincidence that I found my finding only a couple of days later and the fact that it was conceived some fifteen years earlier (and in another country, no less — where said piece of paper should supposedly be, by the way), is *beyond* astonishing — it's... extraordinary. Undeniably serendipitous, for sure. Uncanny, without doubt. Are you thinking what I am thinking? Right? Yep, reality and I still get along quite well.

Days shorten as they get snoozed. And so weeks get snoozed — whole years, if you're not mindful. I'm not. I have so much I want to do. Most of it never leaves the winding confines of my head.

Nobody has ever betrayed me so fully, so wholeheartedly and with such gusto.

The way back home before the way back home. I'm packing. My head's racing. My mind is running circles around my body. If push comes to shove, I'll just shove.

"Life allows for only one harvest" — another one of my dad's pearls, to close the chapter nicely.

CHAPTER WHAT THE...

But I overstayed my welcome in New York. Or I got spat out by the breathing monument. Or I got sickened by my own tiredness. My whispering Babel mistress became too loud for me to not comprehend either her whims nor my own purposes any longer. Time had become still. I left.

I came to the place with the cherubs. This place is jammed with wheeled angels. They are a dime a dozen, and some of them won't cost you more than that dime. Quite literally. Angels here fall from the sky, fall in your lap, fall from grace. They simply fall. And some angels you'll find here — and in other places too, but this is the angelic place — some angels you'll find here have black wings and their skin is of a faint gray tinge. But you won't notice that when you embrace them under the moon and let them have your heart, kiss it; but you will appreciate your predicament better when morning comes and all that is left is your gold in your pocket — which was not what they were after.

And what do you know? Succubus was right. Of "all my friends", all but a handful were to be counted when the time for tallying came. Meanwhile, fingers seemed to be lost in a fortnight.

But subuccuS had long left my bed. The Moon looms.

Two days later, sitting in a large locale I'd visited previously. Faces impersonal but very agreeable.

Eleven years. Numerology comes to mind. Not that I believe in it – or even know how it works. But I know that in numerology numbers are reduced to a single digit. But there's something different about 11 – the single digit reduction doesn't apply. It's supposed to be unique. Well, 22 also, in fact, but fuck 22. Eleven. They talk of struggle, perseverance, challenges, paradoxical lives. Or paradoxical life paths. Eleven years, and as I look up and around, all these faces are as strange to me as mine is to them. Foreign. But it's my eleven years, not theirs. The paradox, to me, is that I wanted 11 to be reducible, just like any other ordinary number. This impossibility is now blanketed in black around me, as witnessed through the walling glass dividing this world from the cooler, colder, unblanketed one beyond the transparent shielding panes.

But the Moon and her righteousness. And being right and wronged. Right, but wronged? Clear vision. Unclouded foresight. Sheer wisdom. Implacable curse. Unwavering course. The Moon orbits high as she tides tall. And she knows all.

As I walk down an empty little asphalt road that crosses a green prairie, I look around, taking in the cloudless, calm loveliness that surrounds me. A weather-aged white wooden fence segregates nature and progress. I stop for a break. I lean up on the friendly fence, put one foot up on one of the planks, and take a cigarette to my lips. Again, I misplaced my Zippo... Here it is: pants, right front pocket. As I ignite it, the glare on the silvery metal surface greatly outshines the flame that's to be expected. I immediately look up, in sync with the blast: in the blue vastness a jet plane has just materialized overhead, as one of its mighty wings has, conversely, just vanished, leaving in its place a huge ball of fire.

I was living in Los Angeles only a few months when I experienced my first big earthquake. They say there are about a

[77]

thousand earthquakes yearly in the city (which averages about three a day), most obviously too minor to be even noticed. As it turns out, I was on the phone when it hit, talking to – of all people – my mother. And I'm engrossed in the conversation, and don't really notice when the light vibration starts. As it progresses, I begin to realize something is a little off (really, Sherlock?). My awareness is now full when the rattling in the cupboard becomes more audible than the sound of my mother's voice. "I think this is an earthquake", I mumble to myself. "Earthquake? Get on the first plane out of this place!", my mom yells back. And all the while I was thinking about the things I was, I guess, supposed to be doing – placing myself under a door frame, etc. – but was too enthralled by the experience to in fact move a single muscle.

That airplane seems so close to me as it spirals out of control that I can almost feel the heat from the flaming fuselage. I've learned my lesson from that earthquake incident, however, and have no intention of staying for the screening of this particular feature. I look up at the unbridled monster, trying to speculate which way it's going; my next step is to run in the other direction. The only problem is that it's bouncing off the walls in the sky as it swivels wildly. I have now wasted close to three precious seconds – which, by the way, seem much longer than that. The aircraft now crosses in front of me from left to right in a blazing beeline before taking a vertical dip and plummeting straight to the ground. This happens in slow-motion, by which time I have already started to run for dear life – just to save time on the about-face procedure, I decided I'd go in the direction I'm already facing. Racing, I look back to witness the metal shrapnel multiply as the one-winged behemoth collides with the earth, mindful that some of it might come in my pursuit. Air and a white wooden fence is all that separates us.

As the airplane was taking its final dive, I noticed more of its brethren laying around in that very field. Steel carcasses were about and abounded, yet I had failed to notice them, had been blind to my surroundings as I walked... Or had I?

Reminiscences aside, this is running time. Fiery frisbees whizz by and massive iron boards wheel past me as I consider how I should've stopped smoking long ago

[79]

– maybe that would now give me a leg up on the competition.

And then all the rumbling ceases, just as suddenly as it started. I glance back to witness the now frozen blaze; it no longer consumes the remains of the aircraft, but rather stands like an edifice of ice. And the burned up, twisted fuselages have become mystifyingly knitted steel monuments. The calm loveliness has returned to the prairie. I have lived to tell the story.

I need to reassess my approach to walking the road, refine my vision. Re-think my thinking. En route for thought.

CHAPTER NEARING THE END

The Boy has had many incarnations. He was born and re-born a few times. In what seems to be his latest incarnation, he's grown to be a man, and he wound up where the angels are said to be. Barns, soccer fields, big apples and everything in between are, at this point, unsung chronicles; they are sometimes recounted anecdotes of past adventures, foreign travels, lost-in-time lovers, a few conquests and losses. The Boy is where the angels are, and this is where he found his own. This is where he encountered The Girl.

Yes, The Girl.

After a brief intermission...

THE FINAL CHAPTER ?

Screenplay
by

Johnny D.

&

Moon T.G.

Based on the novel
(there are novels, and there are novels)

The Dog, the Voice & the Side Road

First draft: 04/06/12
Current draft: 08/07/12

Dog, Voice & Side Road Productions
1 Love Street
(555)555-5555

EXT.(INT.?) EDGE OF THE WORLD - DAY

The SEMI-GLOWING CHILD with semi-catlike
eyes ambles away after sitting THE GIRL
in a waterfall-resembling sofa piece of
furniture -- similar to the one JOHNNY
sits in, right across from her.

Their chairs sit near the edge of a wide
polished rose quartz platform. Behind
them, airborne, flaming trapeze artists
do their thing.

Johnny is still awed by his environment,
but his eyes are on The Girl. And The
Girl's eyes are on Johnny; she seems
unfazed by her surroundings -- she is
all resolve. She's very easy on the eye.

                    THE GIRL
          What the hell is that, Johnny?

She refers to a... to something laying
beside him on the couch.

                    JOHNNY
          The back of my head. Long
          story.

                    THE GIRL
          Well, make it snappy, because
          that's the reason I came all
          the way here.

                       [83]

> JOHNNY
Whatever do you mean, dahlin'?

> THE GIRL
Don't try to charm me with
your poor-ass Doc Holiday
impression.

> JOHNNY
Okay, Moon, why are you here?

> MOON
Because of that.

She points at the piece of his skull by
his side.

> JOHNNY
Oh, this.

Beat.

> MOON
What have you done?

Johnny doesn't have answers; he has
unanswered questions of his own.

> MOON (CONT'D)
Why are you looking at me so
intently, almost like a baby
would?

                    JOHNNY
I'm searching your face.

                     MOON
For what?

                    JOHNNY
For the truth. Trying to
ascertain whether you're
merely asking, or really care.

                     MOON
Any verdict?

                    JOHNNY
Should we get the check?

                     MOON
Stop it. Why did you have to
do this, Johnny? You left
everybody in an upheaval.

                    JOHNNY
You too?

                     MOON
No, not me! Of course me too!
I'm here, aren't I?

                    JOHNNY
I didn't do it to cause any
disruption.

                    MOON
          Why then?

                    JOHNNY
          I wanted to be able to live
          again.

                    MOON
          So you end your life.

                    JOHNNY
          Sounds paradoxical, yes, but
          it bore fruit.

                    MOON
          Meaning?

                    JOHNNY
          I'm happy here. I'm my old
          self. I missed being me.

                    MOON
          I didn't know that I made you
          so miserable.

                    JOHNNY
          You didn't. Your absence did.

Beat.

Moon's eyes fill up with something...
not tears... History. She smiles
broadly, then laughs with abandon.

MOON

The good times... We were sooo
happy. I missed it so much...
            (with a wink)
...well, maybe not as much as
you did, loverboy...

He lets out a big laugh. She joins in.

JOHNNY

Wit, yeah! Too much to miss,
you funny thing. You kill me!

                    INSERT: SPLIT SCREEN

The two sofas are sliding closer to each
other.   (Or are we imagining it?)

MOON

Yes, you seem like your old
self again. You're funny
again. And it's absolutely
exquisite here. And you are
clearly happy.

JOHNNY

Yep, that I am. So you noticed
the neighborhood...

MOON

What am I, blind?
            (deep sigh)
I just wished you were there.

We could maybe have tried
again.

                    JOHNNY
I proposed that. Many times.

                    MOON
But now it can't be...

                    JOHNNY
People postulated that if I
vanished from your world your
interest would peak again.
Point being that people want
what they can't have...

                    MOON
You vanished...

                    JOHNNY
You can't have me.

A beat. A sly smile; four measures of
word, one measure of mischief...

                    MOON
Oh, but I can.

WE PULL BACK...

...to reveal a unified sofa.

                              FADE OUT.

The Boy was where the angels are, and that is where he found his own. That is where he encountered The Girl. And where he lost her.

EPILOGUE

The blue Hellvenian sun starts to rise beyond the purple seascape which has been the backdrop for Moon and Johnny's rendezvous. Contrary to the usual bustle, in these wee hours no one is in sight. All is absolutely quiet, except for the faint crooning of the invisible morning birds.

"Did I kill you, Johnny?" Moon has answers in her eyes.

"You killed the moon, Moon", is his reply.

She speaks, however her lips don't move and the words never come out of her mouth.

She produces a crumpled up piece of parchment paper from her purse. She takes her time smoothing it out. "I've always loved your words. And your wording."

She's on a mission, devoting her full attention to her delicate charge.

"I did a bad thing", she says, finally looking up. "I stole this from your poetry notebook." She takes a long, deep breath, readying herself for the task ahead.

"She had a beautiful, long wake
After the fact, in my mind's eye
Carnations lay along the lake
She gone, I heal, sweet tears I cry

I wasn't there for her funeral
Don't exactly know when she died
Didn't get to see the burial
But I know, just know that she byed"

She puts it back in her purse. But now she folds it carefully. "You wrote a requiem for me —"

"No", says Johnny. "I wrote that requiem for myself. Did you read what's on the other side of that page?"

"Nope", she shakes her head.

"Well, you already stole the damn thing...", he reasons.

She goes back into her purse and retrieves the proof of her crime. She unfolds the paper, flips it over, and cracks a smile as she begins to read.

"I came upon the most exquisite garden
A blued rose stood out from this enchanting nest
Caught is my eye, sweet lock up, sweetest warden
I committed no crime, to all I confessed"

"*This* I wrote for you, gorgeous. My little farewell note." He can see a twinkle in her eyes, and his own eyes

[91]

sigh as deep as they did when he first breathed the scent of her hair.

"*I committed no crime, to all I confessed...*' I love that." Big smile.

The awakening sun casts a faint bluish glow onto the gleaming rose quartz of the platform. The ocean yawns, oblivious to all, and is hushed by a single invisible bird.

Johnny and Moon look at each other until the seconds begin to rust, their eyes seeing what eyes can't see.

"You didn't have to come here, Moon."

"Neither did you, Johnny, but you have, no doubt, concocted in this big noggin of yours an inspirational resort for us to make poetry."

NOTE: All "typos" in this book were intended.